This **World Book Day 20** b
local bookseller, Hodder Chil̶d̶r̶e̶n̶'̶s̶ ̶B̶o̶o̶k̶s̶ ̶a̶n̶d̶
David Almond.

This book has been specially written and published
to celebrate 20 years of World Book Day.
For further information, visit:
www.worldbookday.com

World Book Day in the UK and Ireland is made
possible by generous sponsorship from National
Book Tokens, participating publishers, authors,
illustrators and booksellers. Booksellers who
accept the £1* World Book Day Token bear
the full cost of redeeming it.

World Book Day, **World Book Night** and **Quick
Reads** are annual initiatives designed to encourage
everyone in the UK and Ireland – whatever your age
– to read more and discover the joy of books and
reading for pleasure.

World Book Night is a celebration of books and
reading for adults and teens on 23 April, which sees
book gifting and celebrations in thousands of
communities around the country:
www.worldbooknight.org

Quick Reads provides brilliant short new books by
bestselling authors to engage adults in reading:
www.quickreads.org.uk

*€1.50 in Ireland

For Mike and Sheelagh

ISLAND

DAVID ALMOND

Hodder
Children's
Books

HODDER CHILDREN'S BOOKS

First published in Great Britain in 2017 by Hodder and Stoughton

1 3 5 7 9 10 8 6 4 2

A CIP catalogue record for this book is available from the British Library.

ISBN 9781444937176
Export ISBN 9781444938241

Printed and bound in Great Britain by CPI (UK) Ltd, Croydon, CR0 4YY

The paper and board used in this book are from well-managed forests
and other responsible sources.

The Hachette Children's Group would like to thank Holmen Paper,
Hallsta Mill, Sweden and Paper Management Services for their contribution
to the paper used for this World Book Day printing.

Hodder Children's Books
An imprint of Hachette Children's Group
Part of Hodder & Stoughton
Carmelite House
50 Victoria Embankment
London EC4Y 0DZ

An Hachette UK Company
www.hachette.co.uk

www.hachettechildrens.co.uk

ONE

An early afternoon, late May. I've travelled north all morning with Dad, through endless-seeming drizzle and mist. We curse this northern climate and we cry out for the sun. We're heading towards Lindisfarne. It's also called Holy Island, because of the miracles that were supposed to happen there, for the masterpieces that were created there, for the atmosphere that still lingers there. It's only a real island at high tide. We turn off the bleak A1 and drive between high hawthorn hedges towards the hidden sea. There's still mist and drizzle when we get to the causeway. We've checked the tide timetables and we thought that by now the tide would be out, but no. The water's still high and the causeway's submerged. The island is lost in the mist. There are yellow warning signs. A skull and crossbones. A photograph of a car submerged in the sea, the passengers huddled together on its roof.

CHECK TIMETABLES

BE PATIENT

TAKE CARE

DANGER OF DEATH

Dad parks the car and we wait. Lindisfarne. We've been coming here every year, ever since Mum died. It's a holiday that's also a pilgrimage, a journey into the beautiful past, into the place she loved above all others in the world.

We say we don't mind that we have to wait. We're trying to be at ease with each other, trying to get that Lindisfarne feeling – that happy sad feeling that we know so well. Our bodies lean towards each other. This is my father, the living person I love above all others in the world.

He puts on the radio and immediately there's news of another bomb on a train in France. He grunts and says we don't need that here, not now. He switches through the channels and finds an opera playing. He sighs with delight and does that thing where he sings along with the soprano, laughing as he lifts his voice girlishly high. I used to find it hilarious. The car windows are open and the voices blend with the invisible larks singing above the fields behind and the invisible gulls squealing above the sea ahead.

And the mist disperses as the waters fall.

The drizzle stops.

And the light returns.

And there they are, as they always are, in the world and in my mind: the gleaming sea, the dunes, the rooftops of the village, the castle on its rock, the memories that rise and fall like water, that shift like sand.

Dad sings on. I want him to stop. I want to hear the sea, the birds, the breeze.

I don't hear the boy's footsteps. He's suddenly there by my window and for an instant he pauses. He turns his head and looks into my eyes. His silver earrings shiver and glint. His hair is dark and shining, and it stands up in a crown of spikes around his head. He's dressed in black and he carries a red rucksack. His clothes are dusty and worn. We share that glance, no words. He keeps on moving forward and he wades into the sea. It's ankle-deep, shin-deep. I want to yell out a warning.

'Stupid fool,' says Dad. He raises his voice. 'Hoy! Take your time, son!'

No reaction. And we know there's no real danger, not at this time. He won't be washed away.

Dad shrugs, and leans towards the windscreen.

'Fool. But what a hairstyle, eh? Punk. I thought that had died years back. But mebbe it still exists where he comes from.'

'Where he comes from?' I say.

'Well, doesn't look like he comes from here, does he?'

He laughs.

'I played with punk myself for a while. I wore

nothing but a bin bag for a while. Had a necklace of safety pins. I wrote HATE across my forehead with a Magic Marker. I spat and cursed and snarled and said I detested everything and everybody.'

I roll my eyes: Dad, Head Teacher, in his Levi's and sandals and his red cord shirt and sunglasses, once a punk? No way.

'I was *wild*,' he laughs. 'For a week or two. Probably till your grandma cooked me a chicken pie and asked if I detested that as well. I soon caved in. Takes determination to be a monster …'

He narrows his eyes.

'Where's he from?' he says. 'How'd he get here?'

'We could take him over,' I say.

'Be his ferryman. I think not.'

The water continues falling. There's just an inch or two of it above the causeway. Cars move past us and start to cross. They spray glittering water across the boy as they pass. He takes no notice.

9

Dad switches on the engine and the car rolls forward. We soon catch up with him.

'We could,' I say to Dad. 'You used to hitchhike in your younger days. You told me that.'

He shakes his head.

'That was then. This is now. The world's going through some very dark days. You've got to be careful.'

But he slows down. The boy gazes at me again. A boy? Not quite. A boy becoming a man. There's a tattoo on his cheek, another on his neck. Birds, both of them. On his T-shirt, the two white words: DARK STAR. His eyes are dark dark brown.

I look right into them.

I catch my breath. My heart skips a beat.

Right from that moment, I think that part of me knows what is to come.

Maybe Dad knows something, too. He accelerates quickly, sprays seawater on to the boy, who calls out in protest. I turn to see him with his arm thrust upward, middle finger pointing at the sky, at us. He yells an indecipherable curse.

'Nice boy,' grins Dad. 'I've taught a few like him in my day.'

'I think not, Dad,' I murmur, and he doesn't hear.

I keep turning. The boy diminishes, and becomes a slow-moving dark scratch in the intensifying light.

We drive across the slick wet sands, the draining pools on the causeway, past the refuge hut halfway across, past low-lying dunes, towards the village, the harbour, the castle, the endless sea beyond.

There are swans on the glassy water. Eider ducks paddle by the seaweed. A little flock of terns dances in the sky.

Dad goes on singing. He reaches across and squeezes my shoulder and smiles. I sigh and smile back at him.

Lindisfarne. Yes, I'm glad we came. Good to be here again.

*

My name's Louise. I've just turned sixteen. I first came here when I was two. I have hazy memories of it that might just be dreams: Mum, Dad, me, a sunlit joyful week. Then Mum died when I was eight, in the depths of an icy northern winter, and Dad and I continued coming here. We come to feel her spirit in the island's breezes, in the splash of its sea, the calling of its birds. We always stay at the same place, do the same things. Swim at Snipe Point and Sandham Bay and laugh as we tell each other that the water isn't cold. Eat lobster and cod. Light a fire at night outside our upturned boat-cabin while the firmament intensifies above. Lie in soft pockets of dunes and read to each other from our books. Sing her favourite songs, tell each other each year that our harmonies are becoming more beautiful. Stay at Spinner's Cottage on the lane down to the harbour.

Here it is, the same as always. The bright-green door with the golden Celtic cross as a knocker. The brown mat in the hall with the interweaving complex Celtic pattern on it. Living room with the stove already laid with paper, sticks and coal. The bottle of red wine for Dad, the bag of multi-coloured animal-shaped Haribo for me.

Dad laughs.

'Mrs McTavish thinks you're still eight,' he says.

I'll be eight for this. I rip the packet open and shove a handful of the sticky soft sweets into my mouth. Delicious.

Here's the card that always waits for us.

'Does she hope we have a dazzlingly delicious delightful time?' I ask.

'She does indeed! How on earth did you know? Oh, but look, there is a change!'

And he shows the set of keys left just for me.

'So you're no longer just a little girl to her!'

His eyes linger on me for a moment.

'She's right, of course,' he tells me. 'Not long now until you're a woman, Louise. How quickly all things change.'

I put the keys into my pocket.

He sighs.

'Your mum would have been so proud of you,' he says.

He unscrews the wine, pours himself a glass.

'You're going to say it's six o'clock somewhere in the world?' I say.

'And how did you know that?'

He holds the bottle out towards me and I shake my head.

'Be different if you were with your mates, eh?' he says.

I laugh and think of the wild night last week with Becca and Gem for my sixteenth birthday, getting into bars with fake ID, tottering through Newcastle's streets on charity-shop stilettos. Becca and Gem. They're camping in the Lake District this week. They wanted me to go with them. I said I couldn't. I said the trip to Lindisfarne was really important. I couldn't let Dad down. But I said that one day before too long, maybe when we're at university, we'll all wander the world together. The world will be our oyster. We'll be wandering stars. We'll be footloose and free.

We put our bags into our bedrooms. There's a narrow window that opens to the wide sea. I touch the cold glass, the familiar wooden frame. There's a tiny smiling mermaid lying there as always on the sill. I used to talk to her in the night, I used to swim with her in my dreams. I called her Marina and used to tell myself that she was me.

We'll see seals, maybe dolphins. One year, folk said a family of whales was spotted, out towards Longstone Lighthouse. I peered at the surface of the water all that week, willing the whales to rise and show themselves to me.

Every year I hope they'll rise.

'The usual?' calls Dad. 'Check the shed, walk to the castle then early dinner at the Cuthbert Arms?'

'OK!'

But I hesitate. Another difference this year is my notebook. I write poems, songs, stories in it. I carry it in my rucksack. I never let him see what's in it.

I open it and write.

Hair like a dark jagged gleaming star. Blurred birds on his pale skin. He comes from nothing, from nowhere.

I draw him, too, a jagged figure with his jagged hair.

I close my eyes and there he is, walking across the sea towards me. So strange, how the mind can become a place, a landscape, a whole world. The world within as vivid as the world without.

I draw a straight line for the surface of the water, draw him walking upon it. I draw puffins and terns around his head

The boy, Dark Star, approaches. He seems to be walking from a dream. He seems to be walking on water. There are many birds around his head as well as on his skin. I think he might be very beautiful.

'Ready, Louise?'

'Coming!'

I think he might be terrifying.

*

A flock of puffins dashes by us as we approach the harbour. Little fishing boats tilt on the exposed sand. Seaweed and jetsam on the shoreline. Bits of old net, timber, black weed, plastic bottles, a child's pink shoe. The sand hisses and crackles as the water seeps from it. The lovely sheds: upturned fishing boats, on the turf above the water line. They were hauled from the sea many decades ago, a worn-out herring fleet, when the North Sea was almost emptied of fish. The boats were sawn in half, turned upside down, doors were put on to them, and they became sheds with decks to the earth and keels to the sky.

We go to the shed that comes with Spinner's Cottage. The beautiful curved and pointed shape of it, the black felt roof, the ancient green metal bench outside, the ring of stones for a fire. My heart leaps at the memories and sensations that linger here. Dad un-padlocks the door and we gaze into the shadows and the light. A floor of sand, striped deck chairs, kindling, logs. I step inside, enter the strange baffled silence, breathe the scent of creosote and tar. I tug cobwebs from the tiny window and look through dust and crackled glass out into the endless sky.

'All shipshape?' asks Dad.

'Aye.'

For an instant I hear myself as a child in here. *Daddy! We can sail upside down across the sky!*

I go into the depths of the shed, where the keel curves down to the pointed prow, and there it is, the pencil drawing I made when I was four, the three of us in an upside-down boat surrounded by moons and stars. I'm wearing my favourite red-and-white polka dot dress. Dad calls it my cave painting, created in a distant past, at the very birth of the world. I coloured it in with crayons and it was very bright, almost luminous. I trace it with my fingers. I brush away some dust. Each year it's there, but each year a little more dull, more faded. How old will I be when at last it's gone?

Dad laughs.

'It's still there?' he says.

'Aye.'

'That's good.'

He rattles the keys and we depart.

Families are picnicking by the water. A boy and his father splash in the shallows. A couple embrace on the grass. A group of Japanese tourists step down from a coach. Their guide waves a little flag and they gather around her as she begins to tell what I imagine is a tale of ancient Lindisfarne.

Dad starts to sing the song of two lovers separated by water.

'I cannot get to my love if I would die …'

I take the next line.

'For the waters of Tyne run between her and me …'

We sing together,

'And here I must stand wi' a tear in my ee

'Both sighing and sickly my sweetheart to see.'

We don't need to say anything. We hold hands for an instant and walk towards the castle around the harbour bay. We come to the walled garden below the castle rock. It was established here a hundred years ago by Gertrude Jekyll. Beyond the black steel gate, we sit on a stone seat and praise the growing hollyhocks, the lavender, the espaliered pear trees clinging to the wall. Another of her places. We remember her, we think of her. I take out my notebook and write. He knows not to look over my shoulder.

And Dark Star walks through those memories and thoughts. He is on the island now, his trousers soaked by the sea. He is passing by the window of Spinner's Cottage. I see him there, vivid. His eyes, his hair, the birds drawn on him.

Then Dad takes a cigarette out of a pack and lights it.

'What?' I snap.

He breathes in smoke, blows it out.

'Just for this week,' he says with a shrug.

'You gave up years ago!'

'Yes.'

'Mum would be furious!'

He sighs deeply.

'Ignore it, Louise. Let me relax.'

'Relax!'

I turn my eyes away from him to the sea.

There has been disaster and death. Dark Star has escaped. He has journeyed many months to reach this place of refuge. Here, he will be healed.

The gate creaks open and a woman in a blue dress and running shoes walks in. She reads from a guidebook as she inspects the planting system. Pauses as she passes by.

'Such a beautiful day,' she says.

She looks Asian, has an American accent.

'Oh, it always is, in these parts, pet,' says Dad.

She blinks in surprise, then laughs.

'Ah, English humour of course. I'm still getting the hang of it.'

'And this is English humour with a Geordie touch to it,' says Dad.

'Geordie?'

'Far northern English.' He widens his eyes. 'A bit scary!'

'Yes, you look very scary, sir.'

At the gate, she hesitates. She looks beyond the castle towards the dunes. Mist lingers there, above the track towards the island's wilder parts.

'Is it safe to go that way?' she says.

'Safe?' says Dad.

She's apologetic.

'We hear such stories about how dangerous parts of Europe are these days,' she tells us.

I snort. Dad knocks me with his elbow.

'They're right,' he says. 'That's where the savages are. Do not, whatever you do, go there.'

Her eyes widen, then she grins.

'Ah,' she says. 'English humour.'

'Aye.'

A low-flying jet streaks through the sky over Longstone.

She hesitates again, looks towards the dunes, then turns back towards the village.

Dad watches her, and smiles and smokes.

'Dangerous Lindisfarne!' he says.

'Put that out!' I tell him.

∗

We leave the garden. There are more signs here.

NO CAMPING

NO FIRES

There are photographs of birds, seals, deer.

PROTECT OUR PRECIOUS WILDLIFE

We amble back. Gannets plunge from twenty metres in the sky to kill their unsuspecting prey. Lobster boats bob on the swell. There are more people now, arriving in the cars and tourist coaches that stream across the causeway at every low tide. I keep my eyes peeled, but there's no sign of him.

Three bare-chested teenage lads lounge on and around a metal bench beside the footpath. They're drinking cider, squealing with laughter, effing and blinding.

Dad takes a deep breath and turns all headmasterly.

'Tone it down, lads,' he tells them. 'No need for that in a place like this.'

They go quiet. Two of them look down. One of them blushes. Then the largest steps up to Dad. He has muscles, a six-pack. There's a Union Jack tattooed above his heart.

'What's that you say, old fella?'

'There's children around. People are trying to have a peaceful day.'

'They'll not get that with us around, will they?'

His mates are emboldened. One of them sings softly.

'Get them out … Get them out …'

Dad groans, snaps off his sunglasses, stamps closer to them.

'Don't I *know* you?' he gasps.

The boy snorts. His eyes widen.

'I don't believe it,' he says.

Then he turns and runs.

'Run for your lives, lads!' he yells. 'It's Butcher bliddy Brooks!'

The others scamper after him, swigging cider,

swinging their T-shirts, scattering empty cans.

'I know him,' says Dad. 'I *taught* him. *What was* his name?'

He squeezes my hand.

'You OK, love?'

'Aye. They're idiots, that's all.'

'Monsters, singing things like that to my daughter.'

*

He buys an ice cream, as if to comfort me. I lick it, lick the bright-red monkey's blood on it, feel it seep into me, delicious. Take off my shoes and step across the tender mingle of grass and sand. Close my eyes and feel it between my toes, hear seagulls and exulting larks. Smell sea and seaweed, smell another cigarette burning.

'Anderson!' Dad says suddenly. I open my eyes and turn to him. 'Anderson. That lad. That's what his name was. How could I forget? Jesus, what he did that day.'

'What?' I ask.

'Oh, you don't want to know, Louise. It was

to do with a cat. He …'

But then the Asian American woman is here again with her big eyes and her slender legs. I go back to stepping over the grass and sand. I hear him telling her that we come every year, a sentimental journey. He refrains from mentioning my mum. She says she's on a long-anticipated trip, first to Europe, but her main destination is Vietnam.

'A long journey,' says Dad.

'Yes. I'll take my time, get there slowly. I've waited a whole lifetime for this, and I'm doing it step by step.'

'A pilgrimage?' says Dad.

'You could call it that,' she says.

'Why Lindisfarne?'

'No real reason. I just looked at a map and it seemed to say, *Come here*. Who knows why?'

She tips her head to one side, and they regard each other.

'I'm staying at the Manor House,' she says.

'Nice?'

'Very Olde English. I even have a four-poster bed. It's like sleeping in a galleon.'

He laughs with her.

'The things that entice you tourists,' he says.

Beyond them and between them I see Dark Star coming slowly out of the village. He gazes around, as if seeking his destination, then he heads to the upturned boats, as if that's where he's been heading all this time. And he reaches out and touches our shed, rests his open palm on it. Walks right around it. Stands on tiptoe and peers into the little window. And sits on the bench beside its door.

As if he's at peace.

As if he's quite at home there.

He takes off the rucksack, takes out some bread. He breaks it, and eats. He opens a bottle of dark liquid and drinks. Dad and the woman go on talking.

'That would be all right, wouldn't it?' says Dad.

'What would?'

'If Coral dined with us.'

'Coral?'

'Coral. My friend.'

I blink, can't answer. Would it really?

'She's here on her own,' he continues. 'We could fill her in on some Lindisfarne lore.' He grins at both of us. 'My daughter is called Louise,' he says to Coral.

She puts out her hand. I just look at it, and he laughs, like he used to do when I was an awkward ten-year-old.

'Yes, it would be lovely,' he says, 'and the crab at Cuthbert's, Coral, is delicious.'

They make their date. She walks away in her running shoes.

'*What?*' I say.

'She's nice,' he says. 'I'm sure we'll like her.'

He chews his lips. He watches her as she diminishes. There's a stupid look on his face. My God, how horrible. He bliddy fancies her.

'What about him?' I say. 'I wonder where he's staying?'

He says nothing. I poke him and he comes back to reality.

'Who?'

I gesture towards Dark Star.

'Him. I wonder where he's staying?'

He shrugs.

'Nobody comes to the island with nowhere to stay,' he says. 'Somebody'll chuck him off. What is he? A tramp or something? Asylum-seeker? Nothing to do with us.'

He leans forwards and peers at the boy.

'Wonder what he's seen,' he says. 'Wonder what he's done.'

He strokes his hair, his chin.

'Mebbe I'll have a wash and a shave, love. Change me shirt, eh?'

'Aye. OK. You go and do that, Dad. I'll wander around for a while.'

'Don't get lost.'

He laughs at the absurdity of the idea then walks away, all jerky like a teenager.

*

Still barefooted, I wander aimlessly, make spirals and jagged pathways across this part of the island. And that weird feeling comes, the one I always get when I'm here, like I'm me as I am now, but I'm also every age I've ever been – a baby, a toddler, a girl, a teenager. Then the other feeling comes, the one that sometimes stops me in my tracks, the one about the simple weirdness of being me.

Why am I me, Louise Brooks, and not somebody else?

Why am I not Dark Star or the woman in the garden?

Why am I a human being and not a bird or a fish or a seal?

Why am I alive, not dead?

Why am I not a wave of water, or a rock or an anything?

I asked Becca stuff like that last week and she hooted with laughter.

'*What?*' she giggled. 'Why aren't you a bliddy *pigeon*? Get another Jaegerbomb down yer neck.'

But why? Why does the sun shine and the wind blow and …

No answers.

Such questions have no answers.

So don't ask them, Louise.

But I can't stop asking them.

I'll never stop asking them.

I try not to look at Dark Star, but I know he's still sitting there by the boatshed. At last, I get braver. I pass close by him, and wander down on to the harbour shore and step into the water. It's icy; lovely as it turns, rises and falls over my feet, my ankles, my calves. I feel him there, just a short distance behind me, and it's like there's some strange intensity linking me to him. I stare out at the harbour mouth, the sea beyond, the sharp horizon.

And I get this brand-new weird sensation: I am the island, the island is me. The harbour mouth is my mouth and the sea is turning inside me. And there are fish swimming in me, and seals, and seabirds flying through me. And Dark

Star is inside me as well, like he's some half-known unexpected part of myself that needs to be acknowledged, that needs to be known, that needs to be touched.

I stand in the water.

I am Island.

What would Becca say to *that*?

And then he's at my side, just a few short metres away. He's wading knee-deep into the water with his trousers on and his T-shirt off. And he crouches down and submerges himself and rises again gasping, with the sea draining from him and with the spikes of his hair gone, just dark hair falling smoothly across his scalp and face. He hoots and submerges himself again then rises and stares at me.

And he is beautiful, and strange, and I feel little and inadequate and timid in the shallow sea, but I can't turn away.

'Have you been here before?' I blurt out.

'What? No. How could I have been here?'

'Where will you stay?'

A curlew flies over us. Somewhere, the larks exult.

Maybe he doesn't understand.

'Have you got somewhere to stay?' I ask again.

He wades towards the shallows, towards me.

There's a dark-blue star tattooed on the centre of his chest.

'I don't know,' he says.

His voice is light. He says the words as if he's just learned them, as if he's saying them for the very first time.

'Where do you recommend?' he says.

The answers would be crazy: St Aidan's Hotel; the Manor House with its galleon beds.

'Lost your tongue?' he says.

Suddenly, he reaches down into the water and brings up a little fish that wriggles in his hand. He shows it to me then bends again and lets it swim away.

I don't know what to say, don't know how to ask how he can do such a thing. He laughs at my silence.

'Are you frightened of me?' he says.

'I don't know. I don't think so. Should I be?'

He shrugs.

'I don't know,' he says. 'Many people seem to be. Should I be scared of you?'

Scared of me? Me? Sixteen-year-old Louise? The idea is nonsense.

'Of course you shouldn't be,' I tell him.

He shrugs again.

I look at this boy with tattoos on him, with darkness and trouble and distance and deep calm in his eyes. And I feel so young: that little girl again with her mouth full of Haribo and her dreams of sailing across the sky.

'If you stay until the next tide,' I say, 'you'll have to stay all night.'

He shrugs.

'And it's warm now,' I say, 'but it'll be really cold then.'

'Who?' he says again.

I open my mouth to speak but suddenly my name is on the air, ringing through the empty spaces around our heads.

'Louise! Louise!'

It's Dad, in a yellow shirt and black jeans.

'Louise!'

'You're Louise,' says Dark Star.

'Yes. I have to go.'

'Who is that?'

I look at the distant figure waving me to him. He looks suddenly unfamiliar, a stranger to me, like I don't know him at all.

'It's my dad,' I stammer at last. 'My father.'

And I wade back from the water on to the sandy turf and hurry back towards him.

*

The crab looks and smells delicious. There are wedges of lemon and brown bread and butter with it. But I can't eat, not with her here, not with this woman here on our very first night. They don't notice. They drink white wine and I pour myself a small glass, too. She's wearing a blue top that shows the cleavage between her breasts. I want to take my wine and pour it down there.

Dad tells her that the island has always been a holy place. She pretends she knows nothing as she nibbles and licks and chews and makes eyes at him, as he blathers on about the saints who lived here, about Aidan and Cuthbert and their ancient monastery.

'And are those its ruins?' she says.

She points through the window at the dark stone arch with sea and sky within it. The bare-chested boys are there, leaning against the ruins, smoking.

'No,' he says. 'They didn't make monuments. Their place was made of clay and thatch. It all blew away centuries ago.'

'Blown away into the mists of time,' she intones.

He smiles sweetly, as if he's never heard anything more profound.

'It was a place of miracles and healing,' he says. 'Travellers were given rest here. The poorly and the poor were cared for. It's said it was a kind of heaven, a place and time when men and beasts lived in harmony.'

She sighs.

'Ah, back when the world was young.'

'Yes. Till the barbarians came and ruined everything.'

'The Vikings?'

'Aye.'

He points out towards the sea.

'Narrow your eyes and you can nearly imagine them pouring across the sea in their boats.'

'Monsters,' she sighs. 'Killing, howling, smashing, burning.'

She rests her chin on her hand.

'Maybe all civilisations are destined to end,' she says. 'Maybe the destroyers are always waiting for their chance to move in.'

I watch the bare-chested boys in the ruins. One of them tilts his head back and pours cider into himself. Another of them starts to climb a ruined pillar, shinning his way up until he's higher than a man, then he loses his grip and falls back down. His friends are doubled over in laughter. I hear their hoots. The boy flexes, stretches, and starts to climb again. His friends chant what must be his name, as if they're at a football match. He climbs, then falls again from a greater height. I see a couple of stones from the pillar fall with him.

'Lindisfarne culture wasn't destroyed,' says Dad. 'The Vikings didn't get the book.'

'The famous Lindisfarne Gospels,' she replies.

She digs into her handbag and takes out a tourist guidebook. She shows a copy of a page from the Gospels. It shows St John the Evangelist, writing on a scroll with an eagle leaping from his haloed head. I lean forward. Oh, yes. It truly is a masterpiece. This is what I'd like my notebook to be like. But I see myself in place of St John. I see skylarks in place of the eagle. I see my own jagged spiky urgent writing.

Dad's hand touches Coral's as they reach out to trace the page's beauty.

'They saved the book,' he says. 'They carried it away along with the body of St Cuthbert. They said that when they took his body out of his grave, it was uncorrupted, as if he'd only been sleeping.'

'Could that be true?' asks Coral. 'That the dead may only be asleep?'

'Who knows?' says Dad. 'Anyway, they saved him and the book from the barbarians. Civilisation went on.'

The boys are chanting and hooting again. She shows another page. The gorgeousness of it. The beauty of the patterns around the words. The strangeness of the stylised beasts and birds that live at their edges. I imagine such pages made by myself. I imagine Dark Star upon them, wandering around the words, folded into the words.

'Blessed are the merciful,' she reads, 'for they shall receive mercy.'

'I used to read that to the children in my school.'

'To keep them on the right path,' says Coral.

'Yes.'

'Did it work?'

He smiles.

'Ah, for those that had ears to hear, perhaps.'

'What about that boy?' I say.

'Which boy?' he says.

I roll my eyes and point towards the ruins.

'Him out there. The one who told me to get them out, Dad. The one you were going to tell me about.'

'Ah yes, him. Anderson. He was young. They're all still young. They'll grow up, they'll change.'

'Will they?'

*

They eat and drink and gaze into each other's eyes.

The light outside softens, becomes golden.

In the restaurant there are animal skulls hanging on the walls. Stuffed fish in glass cases on tables. Stuffed birds on shelves. Horrible. I turn my gaze from the light outside to the dark cavity in a skull where a deer's eye once was.

'You can still feel the holiness and peace in the very air,' says Coral.

'Can you really?' I say.

'Yes, it doesn't go away. It cannot be destroyed. Don't you feel it, too, Louisa?'

'Louise.'

'Sorry. Louise.'

'No, I can't,' I say.

I don't want her to feel that we share any thoughts, any reflections.

I don't want her to feel that she has anything to do with me.

'It's like a body,' I say suddenly, surprised myself at the thought.

'What is?' asks Coral.

'The book. The Gospels. They're made of skin. The skin of calves. And the words and pictures were marked on the skin. The book is like a body with writing on it. The words are like tattoos.'

Her eyes are dead and empty as she listens.

Dad grins.

'Teenage girls, eh?' he says. 'This lass has always been one for the weird theories.'

He pours her more white wine. She swirls it around her glass and sips it with her pink lipsticked lips. She tugs her top and her breasts tremble.

'And it's like it's still alive,' I say. 'Dead, but still alive.'

She makes that noise again.

'I mean it's still speaking to us,' I say. 'It's still showing us its beauty.'

I lean closer to her.

'Can you not see that?' I ask her, like I actually mean, *How can you be so bliddy stupid?* 'It's like nothing ever really dies,' I tell her. 'Nothing's ever destroyed, once it's turned to art.'

She says nothing.

I pour another glass of wine for myself, and her empty eyes widen in surprise.

'Is that wise?' she asks Dad.

'Wise?' he asks.

'In the USA, you'd be locked up for letting

your child drink wine.'

I laugh. She stares at me.

'Not here,' I tell her. 'I was paralytic in Newcastle last week. I honked up in a rubbish bin outside Burger King.'

'*Louise!*' says Dad.

'You know it's true, Dad. I was dead to the world, then I had a hangover that lasted three whole days.'

The woman sighs. She mutters something.

'What?' I ask her.

'I said it seems so uncivilised,' she says.

I snort.

'Uncivilised? You're calling me uncivilised? You from the place where you shoot each other in the streets, from the place where you think you have the right to bomb the world?'

'Louise!' says Dad.

He glares at me.

'She doesn't mean it,' she says.

'She does!' I say. 'Bliddy Americans. Bliddy barbarians. All the same.'

'I'm not just American,' she says. 'I'm half Vietnamese.'

I take no notice. I gulp my wine. I hate this stupid dull woman. I want to bring Becca and Gem here and show her how mental we all are. I want to be in the Lake District with them, walking in the hills, looking at lads, downing cider.

The woman regards Dad with sympathy. Poor man, to have such a wayward daughter. He grins sweetly at her. He even blushes. For God's sake. What's wrong with the stupid man?

He pours her more wine. Now he's telling her about my mum and her too-early death. Her eyes brim with tears as she says that sounds so sad. She looks at me and I can see her thinking that it explains a lot about me. She touches his forearm for a moment, and leans closer to him. Must be so difficult, bringing up a child alone. Must be so difficult, keeping her on the straight and narrow.

I hate her. How dare she pass judgement about my mum and me like that? How dare my dad allow her to?

There's more fish, pieces of salmon and cod on a shared plate. There's potatoes and salad and more bread. I pick at a potato.

Outside, the day visitors are leaving. Buses filled with tourists head back towards the causeway. The shadows lengthen. The boys are gone from among the ruins. I can't see Dark Star. I squint, peer, try to focus.

She's telling him something about friends and family she's lost, too. She's saying something about Vietnam. She's saying that sometimes it seems that death is all around us, like the world is a zone of death.

Dad sighs like that's really profound, like he's never heard anything so clever.

'I guess the lesson is,' she says, 'that we must live each day as if it is our last.'

'*Carpe diem*,' I say.

'Pardon?' she says.

'*Carpe diem*. It's Latin. Seize the day. Do what you want to do now.'

She widens her eyes.

'You have such a clever daughter, Robert,' she says.

Dad leans closer to her with his eyes glazed over. I see him taking it all in, her hair, her eyes, her lips. His gaze lingers on her breasts. She tells him that she'll only be here a day or two and then she'll be gone. He tells her that is such a shame. So much to see here, Coral, so much to learn. He takes no notice of, or doesn't see, my cold stare.

She strokes her cheek.

'*Carpe diem*,' she murmurs.

'YOLO,' I say.

'What? Is that Latin too?'

'No. It's Geordie. It means the same thing. YOLO. You Only Live Once. So live your life now.'

'I will take that advice,' she says.

I'm starting to cry and I don't want them to see. I push my plate away.

'I'm off,' I say.

'Maybe that's for the best, Lou,' he says. 'Get

away on your own for a while.'

I stand up. Their faces are almost touching.

'Stop it!' I snap.

They both flinch.

'You're supposed to be here with me!' I say.

'Oh, love,' says Dad.

He reaches towards me. I back away.

The woman just contemplates me with big stupid compassionate-looking eyes.

'I'm off,' I tell them again.

They don't try to stop me.

Dad just softly says, 'Don't go too far.'

I pass by a line of dead fish and I leave.

*

I cast them out of my thoughts. The light is beautiful. The sky over the sea to the east is a mingling of pink and blue with long stretches of white mackerel cloud upon it. I throw my arms wide at another weird thought – fish in the sky above, fish in the sea beneath, fish joining everything to everything.

I walk towards that sky along the path by the

castle, past the walled garden towards the wild places. A family runs past me towards the harbour and the car parks. The mother's snapping at her children.

'Hurry up! Hurry! We'll miss the tide! We'll all be drowned!'

There's panic in the children's eyes.

'You'll be fine!' I shout after them.

'How do *you* know?' snaps the woman. 'Hurry, children. Hurry!'

I walk with long strides. I throw my arms wide to the sky. Sometimes I feel I could fly when I'm here, that I could just step up into the air, keep stepping up into the sky until I can look down upon everything, upon this island. This zone of my childhood, this sanctified place.

I slow down and amble to long grass, towards the dunes beyond Emmanuel Head, I catch my breath, become dead still. The deer are there, a little family of them. They're the only deer on the island. We were told that they arrived last year, were seen one moonlit night making their way across the causeway. Their heads turn towards me. Do they smell me? Do they see me? Do they think I'm danger? I try not to breathe, try to calm my thumping heart. They're so beautiful, those wide eyes, tender faces. They're as still as me. Then suddenly they turn and leap away and their bodies are arched and stretched as they bound from the earth and through the sky. They pause, a hundred yards away, and turn to look at me again. Checking that I haven't sprung after them? Or inviting me to follow them? Then they leap again and disappear. Lovely beasts, so timid, so tender, so wild. Farewell.

*

I walk on, with the thrill of the deer still inside me. I know Mum is here, in the air, the light, the atmosphere of this place. Sometimes I see her. I told Dad that a couple of years back and he just murmured, 'Yes, I'm sure you do. It's natural, Louise.' He didn't understand. I do see her. It's not like seeing a ghost. It's not something weird or scary. It's like she's there drifting at the edge of my vision, in one of the long floaty dresses she loved so much, like she wanders somewhere at my side and sometimes shows herself. Just a glimpse. She's here now as I come to the long white beach where I've swum so often with Dad. A presence in the air, on the breeze, a presence carried on the light.

'Hello, Mum,' I whisper.

*

The surf turns gently as the tide rises. I'm suddenly a toddler again. I remember her carrying me to the water all those years ago. I remember the strength and comfort of her hands and arms, I remember being cradled against her as she waded in waist-deep, and lowered me in, held me on the surface.

'Welcome to the sea, my canny bonny bairn,' she whispered sweetly into my ear. 'Welcome to the sea, my lovely little mermaid.'

I whispered something in return. Something quiet and intense. The simple word I whisper now:

'Mammy. Mammy …'

I remember how she loved the sea, how she'd run down across the soft sand, and plunge into it. I remember the beauty of her body, the strength and animal vigour of it. I cast my eyes about. The beach is deserted. I strip down to my underwear and I do as she did. I run recklessly and I plunge in and swim down beneath the bitter waves.

The icy shock of it.

The joy of it.

The freedom of it.

'Look at me, Mammy!' I call.

I burst into the air and quickly swim out twenty metres and then back again. I'm hooting at the cold. I stride back out on to the land. She's before me in the dunes, she's behind me in the sea. She is everywhere on Lindisfarne, everywhere inside me.

I swing my arms and dance on the sand to dry myself and to warm myself. I put my clothes back on. I sit at the edge of the dunes and write.

I write the word MUM and at the edge of the page I draw the floating folds of her dress. I draw the shape of the island with the sea around it as if I'm looking down upon it.

The island seems to be floating. The whole world seems to be floating. I seem to be floating.

Then the bare-chested boys are here, coming out from the dunes twenty metres away. They're hooting, cursing, chanting. I close the book. The boy with the Union Jack tattoo, Anderson, comes closer, silhouetted against the sky.

'Let's have a look, then,' he says.

His friends snort.

'Get them out, get them out,' one of them starts.

Anderson laughs.

'No, I mean the book, man!' he says. 'For starters, anyway.'

I put the book into my sack and pull the sack on to my back and walk away serenely. Their hoots and laughter follow me. A stone thuds on to the sand behind me. I turn and make a face of contempt.

I spit salty spit. I spit again, as if I am spitting the boys out from the island that is me. I do not want such hateful things inside me. I want seals and fish and deer and skylarks and upturned boats and clear salty air and I want the presence of my mother and the mystery that is Dark Star.

*

How pathetic he seems, my father, when I see him with this woman. I want to disguise him, to put him into different clothes, to make him walk differently and speak differently, to put make-up and a false beard on his face, so that he's simply some old fool dazzled by an American tourist in a low-cut dress.

I pause by the walled garden as they amble hand-in-hand on the harbour wall in the gorgeous late light. They sit on a harbour bench. They lean close. They kiss. They don't see me, don't look for me, don't care that I might see them. I spit. The sun is molten as it falls across the Cheviots. An almost-invisible moon has risen over the sea. How can they kiss like that? It should be me and people like me who kiss. Like last week in the park, still hungover, me and Kevin Elliott under an apple tree at dusk, tongues deep inside each other's mouth, kissing and kissing and kissing and kissing till we nearly didn't exist, till we nearly disappeared. We looked at each other in amazement afterwards.

'Where have we been?' I whispered.

'Dunno,' said Kevin. 'But let's go back there again soon.'

Kevin. We'd been dancing around each other for weeks without doing anything. Becca could see it. 'Just go for it,' she told me. 'He fancies you. He's told me so. Just try him out.' Just try him out. Is that what you do? Is that what Mum did with Dad? Is that what Dad's doing now? Is that what *carpe diem* means? Kevin. We passed each other at the park gates. Each of us was alone. 'I was just going in for a wander,' he said. 'Want to come with me?' We went inside together. We didn't need to say anything. We just went straight to the apple tree and leaned against its trunk and started as the sun went down and the moon came up. So delicious. *Carpe diem.* YOLO.

Dad and Coral kiss again, then get up from the bench and walk onward, presumably towards her room. I watch them disappear, lost behind the boatsheds, lost in the village streets, lost in the entrance to the Manor House, lost behind the curtains of the four-poster galleon bed.

My phone buzzes. A text.

I might be a little late tonight, love xx

I'm fine, I text. *Be as late as you want xx*

*

Dark Star has lit a fire of driftwood in the circle of stones. He has three fish on a broad flat stone that rests among the flames. They sizzle, blacken, smell delicious.

'You could have one,' he tells me. 'They are nearly done, Louise. They will be delicious.'

'I could bring some bread,' I say.

'Yes.'

So I run to Spinner's Cottage. I get the loaf and a bottle of water left for us by Mrs McTavish and I hurry back again. I sit on the sand. He cuts the bread with a little sharp knife. He lays a fish on a slice for me. A mackerel, my favourite. I nibble the firm oily flesh, I bite into the bread. Yes, so sweet, so salty, so delicious. So simple. Yes, this is what I want: simplicity, beauty, a simple fish with a beautiful boy. Fish in the sky above, fish in the sea beneath, fish inside my belly.

Then I notice the blood on his brow, a dried trickle beneath a small cut. I point to it.

'What's that?' I ask.

He traces it with his finger, inspects his finger, shrugs.

'Blood,' he says. 'Nothing.'

'What happened?'

'Nothing. It happens sometimes, Louise.'

He points to a scar on his forearm, another on his cheek.

'This in Italy,' he says. 'This on a train in France. It's nothing. What would a life be without wounds and scars?'

I want to ask more but he shakes his head.

'It's nothing. It's just that some people do not want a wandering boy wandering among them.'

I ponder my own scars. One on my knee where I fell off my bike, one on my nose from chicken pox. And the internal scars, and the everlasting yearning for a lost mother. And the pain that goes with such scars.

'I think you are a sad girl, Louise,' Dark Star says.

'What?' I answer. I've almost forgotten he's there. 'No, of course I'm not.'

He smiles.

'I am in fact a very happy girl,' I say.

'That's good. It is good to be happy.'

And I am. It's true. It is my wandering weird mixed-up mind that gives the illusion that I am sad. I love my life, I love my friends, I love this world. And scars help me understand how blessed I am.

There are people ambling past. Over the years, we have come to recognise many of those who live here. A fisherman carries a lobster pot, silhouetted against the darkening sky. He waves and smiles.

'No dad this year?' he calls.

'Oh, yes!' I answer.

He gives Dark Star a long hard look, and then moves on.

'Where are you from?' I ask Dark Star.

'From far away, Louise. From somewhere you have never heard of.'

He bites the fish and bread, licks his fingers, swigs the water. He passes the water to me. I swig and try to taste him in it.

He offers me the third fish. I decline. He begins to eat.

'I am from the desert,' he says.

The word in this place seems so intense, so out of place.

'The desert?' I echo, and the word feels strong and strange on my tongue and breath. 'Which desert?'

'The Syrian desert.'

'Ah, of course I've heard of that.'

'Yes. So have you been there?'

'Oh no.'

'It is where the palms bloom and the sun blazes and the air is dry and earth is fierce against the feet. And it is not unlike this place.'

'What?'

'It is beautiful. The sky is wide. It opens the soul.'

I look at his meagre possessions: the rucksack, the knife, some clothes. I think of him walking across the wide world all alone.

'The endless sand is like the endless sea,' he says. 'And the sky is endless everywhere. It makes us know that we are very small. And it has its lovely remnants of an ancient age.'

'Are you a refugee?' I ask him.

'Is that what you would like me to be?'

The question embarrasses me.

'No,' I say.

'I don't know,' I say.

He laughs.

'I am a refugee!' he says. 'Help me! Save me!'

He stands up, puts down his food, and walks a few steps towards the beach. He casts himself down on to the line of jetsam and he lies sprawled there, as if he's been washed up, as if he's drowned, as if he's dead. He doesn't move. Nor do I. A man walking his dog pauses, recoils, walks on.

Dark Star rises again and returns to me.

'Is that how I should be?' he says. 'Thrown up dead on to the shore by the careless sea? Washed up to be mourned and soon forgotten?'

'Of course not,' I answer.

'How old are you?' he asks.

'Sixteen.'

'Where is the man you were with?'

'My father.'

'Yes, you said that. Your father. He does not look like you.'

'Of course he doesn't look like me!'

I look into Dark Star's eyes. I see something wild there, something of myself there. I shiver.

'He'll be coming for me soon,' I say.

'Ah, to save you perhaps. To rescue you from the scary stranger. Are you frightened of me?'

'No. I don't know.'

'I am from Syria, from the desert, from the city of Palmyra. Do you know the city of Palmyra?'

'No.'

'Once it was a major city of the world. A place of temples to the sun and moon and of great archways curving against the desert sky. A place of trade, where all races lived as one. Then it fell as all civilisations can seem to fall. It was destroyed, its people were put to death.'

'That's terrible.'

'The destroyers were the Romans, those thought to be the great civilisers of the ancient world.'

'You lived among the ruins?'

'No, in the modern city by the ruins. The place where tourists stayed when they came to see the great temples and baths and cemeteries that survived, to see the art that was saved from

61

destruction and that lived on through the centuries.'

'It must have been beautiful.'

'Yes. As beautiful as this place, Louise. It was the place where I was born, the place in which I was a child, the place in which I grew.'

He stirs the embers of the fire with a stick.

'And then destruction came again,' he says. 'Bombs fell down on us, tanks and soldiers came. We cannot be allowed to live in peace. We fled like beasts in terror.'

And I remember what happened in this city of Palmyra just last year. The destroyers, blowing up the temples, blasting them to smithereens, turning them to sand and dust.

'Yes,' I gasp. 'I saw it on TV. I saw the temple blown to bits.'

'Ah. Yes. On TV, Louise. You have just remembered. That is good.'

He stirs the embers again. They burn and glow more brightly as the day comes to a close. He throws on a piece of driftwood and it flares to life.

'You are beautiful, Louise,' he says.

I don't know how to answer. I don't know if I should leap to my feet and run from him as a deer would.

'One day,' he continues, 'I will go back to the place of my childhood, just as you come back to Lindisfarne, and it will be a place of happiness and peace again.' He laughs. 'Some would say that is a crazy dream. It is not a crazy dream.'

Suddenly, he stands on his hands. He walks on them around the upturned boatshed. He jumps up on to the keel of the shed and spreads his arms wide and stands there silhouetted against the sunset.

'I am Dark Star,' he says. 'I am free. I wander the world at will. I go where I wish. Who is there to stop me?'

He jumps down again. He turns a somersault.

'Who is there to stop me, Louise?' he asks.

'Nobody. Not me.'

'That's good. I am Dark Star. I come from an ancient family who make tents for those who roam the valleys and the deserts. My tent is my skin. I go where I will and one day I will go to Palmyra again. Do I frighten you, Louise? Do you think I am wild?'

I cannot speak. I feel my mother's shade nearby. I imagine my stupid father with his stupid woman in her stupid bed. I feel suddenly at home with this strange and beautiful Syrian boy.

The air is becoming chill as darkness comes on.

My mind is seething, reeling.

The sea is still, the island is still.

The complex firmament is studded with the very first stars.

I take the keys from my pocket and un-padlock the door of the upturned boat.

Red light shines through the cracked and dusty window on to the sandy floor, into the strange baffled silence.

'You can sleep in here tonight, Dark Star,' I say. 'You'll be safe in here.'

He stands at the door with me.

'It's good to be here at last,' he murmurs.

'What do you mean, at last?'

'It is good to be in a home that is like a boat. A boat that is like a tent. Maybe it will carry me back to Palmrya in my dreams.'

'I could bring you a blanket,' I say.

He shakes his head and takes out a fleece from his rucksack.

'The world's travellers must always be prepared,' he says.

He gazes at me. The late light catches his earrings, his eyes.

'*Carpe diem*,' I whisper inside myself. 'YOLO, Louise.'

I start to shiver.

I am drawn towards him, but I step away from him.

'Now I have to go,' I tell him.

'Yes?'

'Yes.'

He smiles, steps inside, and I leave him.

I hurry away towards the village, in excitement, and not a little fear.

*

I come back here, to Spinner's Cottage on this northern island where the saints once lived, where miracles were performed, where travellers were welcomed, where the sick were healed and a masterpiece was made. This place where my mother lingers and young Louise still walks. I open the door and come inside. Dad isn't here. I lock the door. I find the wine and pour a glass.

I sit by my bedroom window sipping wine, looking out into the night.

I open my notebook and write the words that describe and construct my day.

The village is very still. Somewhere someone is playing the Northumbrian pipes, some sweet lament that merges with the turning of the sea. I would like the words I write to be like that music. I would like my words to be like the cries of those late oystercatchers.

Around the words I scratch drawings of beasts

and birds. Birds fly and fish swim between the lines. I draw a pattern of stars. I draw jagged monsters at the fringes.

I listen to the night. I look out at the stars and sickle moon. The firmament is blazing. The Longstone Lighthouse turns and turns. Darkness then light. Darkness then light. The sea rises, falls, rises, falls. Mind moves and shifts through memories, facts, imaginings and gathering dreams. The time of the night, the condition of the mind, where what is real and what is dream seem to merge into each other, confuse each other. Dark Star is inside the boatshed, inside my mind, deep inside my heart.

I sip the wine.

Somewhere far away there's a frantic animalistic howling.

TWO

I'm woken by footsteps in the street outside at four a.m., then the key scratches in the lock. Dad creeps in, trying to be silent like a guilty teenager, crawling into his bed in the room next door. I look out into the night and catch a glimpse of a pale dress caught in the moonlight. What on earth can Mum think of the man she loved? I doze and dream then must properly sleep at last, for when I wake the sun is burning at the curtains, there are voices in the street, I smell bacon frying.

In the kitchen, he is all jolliness and bright good-mornings and asking what I'd like to do today.

I ignore his question. I eat my sandwich,

drink my tea.

'Coral is staying an extra couple of nights,' he says.

He leans close to me, touches my hand.

'She's very nice, Louise,' he says.

'I don't want to know, Dad,' I tell him. 'I gave the traveller shelter.'

He doesn't listen.

'Coral is an extraordinary woman,' he says. 'Can I tell you about her, about why she is going to Vietnam?'

I ignore that. I tell him again: I gave the traveller shelter.

He doesn't understand, of course.

'Dark Star,' I say.

'The boy we saw on the causeway?'

'Yes, he had nowhere. I let him sleep in our boatshed.'

'You did *what*?' he says.

I just gaze back at him.

'You can't do that,' he says.

'He has to be warm. He has to be safe. It is our

duty to be civilised.'

'To be civilised?'

'Yes.'

'But what has he to do with you?'

'Mum would do it. You know she would. If someone needed help, she'd give it to them.'

'But not somebody like …'

'Like what?'

'Somebody you know nothing about. Some weird-looking wanderer. He could be *anything*, Louise.'

'*Anything*?'

'You know how the world is now. You know the crazy things that are happening …'

He stops and peers closely at me.

'You haven't *done* anything with him, have you?' he says.

'Ha!' I snort. 'That coming from a man who's just slept with a total stranger in a ridiculous bed!'

'Oh, Louise.'

'Yes. Oh, Louise. And I wonder what Mum

would think about *that*!'

He snorts in anger.

'Come on, Louise. Grow up.'

'That's what I'm doing, Dad.'

'Maybe Mum would want me to move on. You know there have been others.'

'Yes, but not in this place. Not when you're with me. Not when her soul is all around.'

'Her *soul*?'

'Yes. Not that you would recognise it.'

'Oh, Louise.'

He reaches out to me but I back away.

He makes his sad compassionate face.

'Oh, love,' he says. 'Don't be so upset.'

I swig the last of my tea and go out into the morning. Am I so upset? No, not really. Just irritated. Disappointed by how easily he's been flattered and seduced. Silly man. Silly father. I keep on walking. Let him do as he wishes. I don't want to be with him. I could have been camping with Becca and Gem. But I'm free to be myself, and to be with Dark Star.

He's outside the shed. His hair is arranged into a halo of spikes again. A little group of folk have gathered around him. He's performing for them: somersaults and headstands and walking on his hands. He cartwheels right across the keel. People clap and gasp. He cups his hands, holds them out, and people drop coins in. He places the coins on a stone outside the boatshed door.

He sees me approaching and he smiles.

'My friend has come,' he tells the onlookers.

They turn to me and separate to let me through and I find myself moving to his side.

'This is Louise,' he tells them.

He suddenly peers at me in surprise.

'I think,' he says, 'that I came here to this island because of this Louise.'

There's a sigh of wonder, even some applause.

He cups his hands where the coins were, closes them, holds them up to the sky, opens them again, and a little bird flies away from them on frantic wings.

More sighs, more gasps, more wonder, more coins.

Dark Star gazes intently at his audience. I see how they are entranced by him, how they want to be entranced by him.

'In the deserts,' he says, 'I travel to the marketplaces and oases. That is where I perform, with the snake charmers and the acrobats and the singers and the storytellers. It is said that the dead wander in such places, that they mingle with the living to be entertained.'

He peers into his little crowd.

'Are the dead among us now?' he asks.

He points to a little boy with an ice cream.

'Are *you* alive, my little friend?' he asks. 'Or are you a ghost?'

He leans close to the boy.

'Look into my eyes, little boy,' he says. 'Tell me that you are not a ghost.'

The boy is speechless. His mother giggles, but puts a protective arm around him.

'I at least,' says Dark Star, 'am truly alive!

Look how I can leap!'

He turns a cartwheel, leaps a somersault.

'I bring the desert to this northern place,' he says. 'To this holy Lindisfarne. I bring the South to the North, the far-flung desert to the far-flung sea.' He laughs and steps towards his audience, holding out his hands. 'And you must give me coins for this, my friends.'

They give him coins. He places them on the stone.

He picks a pebble from the earth and swallows it. He swallows another and another. He regurgitates them and shows them in his hands.

He asks for more coins. He gets them. He laughs.

'Soon I will be rich,' he says. 'But now to stop. Now to feed myself to ward off death. And to spend time with Louise.'

No one moves. He glares at them.

'Away, you ghosts!' he snarls, and laughing they all leave.

*

'Are you OK?' he asks me when they're all gone and we're alone and sitting on the bench outside the shed.

'Yes,' I lie.

'She wants me back,' he says.

'Who does?'

'My mother. And my sister.'

I am mystified.

'I said I would come as far as this and then I would return to them.'

'To Syria?'

'No. That would be impossible. They are in Italy, in Milan.'

'You didn't want to stay with them?'

'We escaped from Syria and came to Italy. They are with some friends. I needed to keep on travelling, to keep on moving to the north.'

'How long have you been away from them?'

'Three months. No, four. They must worry that I am gone for ever. I have performed in Rome, in Barcelona, in Amsterdam, in London, in many places. But this is as far as I will go. My turning point.'

'Why Lindisfarne?'

He's silent. He sighs. He shrugs. He peers into my eyes.

He laughs, suddenly, dismissively.

'Because of you!' he says. 'Just as I told those people!'

'Oh, aye!' I say. 'I'm sure *that's* true!'

'It is!'

We laugh together.

'And I think,' he says, 'that it will be very cold if I go further north as summer ends.'

'It'll be absolutely bliddy freezing!'

'Bliddy. What a lovely word. It will be absolutely bliddy freezing! I need the southern sun! And she wishes me of course to go to university.'

'To university?'

'Ah, you think a tattooed child of the desert, one who eats pebbles and conjures fish and birds, should not be one for university?'

'Of course not, Dark Star.'

'I will go to study in Paris.'

'That's brilliant.'

'I will study history. Perhaps I will become a teacher.'

'Like my father.'

'Ah, he is a teacher? Good. And I also will write about the city of Palmyra, how the roads from it lead back through time, and forward to the whole world, to Lindisfarne and to Louise. I will teach children that they must be very careful in the way they grow up. They must not stop being children even when they are adults. They are the ones who must change the world.'

I shift away from him on the bench. I don't know how to feel about this boy, about anything. I don't know how this is happening. I don't even know if this is happening at all. I catch a glimpse of a dress moving in the breeze nearby and I feel a sudden sense of comfort.

'How old are you?' I ask him.

'Eighteen. No, nineteen. I turned nineteen as I hitchhiked a lift in a lorry at midnight last Friday.

Most people here are very kind. They have carried me a long way.'

'Most people?'

'Yes. The world is balanced between the bad and the good, Louise, between the bitter and the kind. The good and the kind are the strongest, even though they have fewer bombs and swords. Do you know we come from stars?'

He laughs at my silence.

'Every atom in your body was born in a dying star. Truly we are stardust. That is how far we come. We are young and we are as ancient as the universe. Our particles will return again to the universe when we are gone and new children will be made from them. We are all wanderers and travellers, refugees and pilgrims until we return once more to the stars. That is true history. That is true magic. What I do with fish and birds and stones is fancy tricks.'

'Do you believe that the dead walk with the living?' I say.

He shrugs.

'I do not know. But stars are with us. Why not also the dead?'

He gazes at the sea, the air, as if searching for something in them.

I want to tell him about Mum, that I can glimpse her nearby.

'You must feel so far away,' I say to him. 'From your home, from your mother. You must miss her, she must miss you.'

'We always miss the ones we love.'

'Always?'

'For we cannot be with them always, so we miss them even when we are with them, for we think of when we must leave.'

He takes off his Dark Star T-shirt. He exposes the star tattoo at the centre of his chest. He points to it.

'This is the star at the centre of the universe,' he says. 'Wherever I go in the tent of my skin, I am at the centre.'

He laughs softly. I look at the star, at his skin, at his chest. He is very beautiful. *Carpe diem*. I reach out and dare to touch the star with my fingertip, and I feel his skin, the flesh beneath, the bone beneath. He smiles, crouches, and dips his finger into the ash left by last night's fire, then he reaches out and makes a mark with the ash at the base of my throat, the top of my chest. I feel the gentle scraping of the ash against my skin. He's making a star shape, I can tell.

'Now you also are Dark Star, Louise,' he says. 'You also are centre, wherever you wander, wherever you are, however far away you are from those you love.'

He smiles.

'You are centre of the universe, Louise. And you are a pilgrim of the universe.'

I look into his eyes. He looks into mine. I look into the South. He looks into the North. We are balanced. We are in equilibrium.

'Get yer mitts off her!'

It's the boys from yesterday. They're at the edge of the water, in cut-off jeans and flip-flops, tins of cider in their hands.

'Did ye hear? Get yer scruffy mitts off her!'

The boy with the Union Jack tattoo.

'She's not for the likes of you. This is civilisation, pal.'

His companions hoot with laughter.

'Get back to yer hole in the desert and find yer own tart there.'

Dark Star turns away from me and towards them. He reaches down to the earth, picks up sand, cups it in his hands, raises his hands to the air, and casts a little bird into the sky.

They're unimpressed.

'He's a wizard, lads!'

'He's Aladdin!'

'He's a bliddy genie!'

'We'll stuff him back into his lamp!'

Then they back away.

'It's the butcher, boys!'

Dad is here, with the woman linking his arm. The boys pretend to be terrified. They splash their way around the harbour shore, heading back towards the dunes.

'Take no notice,' says Dad. 'They're monsters.'

'We thought you might like to come walking with us,' says the woman.

'No,' I tell her.

'There was talk of dolphins on the far side,' says Dad.

I shrug. Dolphins. So? Maybe they were there, but they'll be long gone by now, ocean travellers.

'No,' I say again. 'I am with my friend.'

The woman whispers something to him. He steps closer.

'Who are you?' he says to Dark Star.

'I am from Palmyra in Syria.'

'How did you get here?'

'I have been travelling. I travelled north, like you.'

'Why are you here?'

'That is the question we all must ask ourselves. That is the question for which there is no answer.' He steps closer to Dad. 'Unless *you* know the answer to this question. Do you know?'

'I am here on holiday,' Dad says. 'I have come

here for Louise and for her mother.'

'Is that why you are here in this universe?'

Dad rolls his eyes at the words. Then he sees that Dark Star is serious. He sighs and ponders. He is intrigued by this boy with his thoughts and questions. He widens his eyes and stares into the sky.

'That's a big question,' he says. 'Why is there a me in this universe? And there's no answer, but it is the kind of question we must ask ourselves, time and again.' He steps closer. I see his eyes softening. This is the Dad I love, the Dad who is the teacher, the Dad who takes all young people seriously, the Dad who believes that young people ask the most important questions. I want to reach out to him, to hug him. I want him to be this Dad. I want him to show his true worth, his true nature, to this dull woman who has so quickly lured him in.

'This place is a good place to ask such questions, Dark Star,' he says

'It is,' says Dark Star. 'Maybe that is why I

have come to this place. Maybe that is why I am here.'

They watch each other.

'Have I seen you before?' says Dad. 'It's crazy. I can't have taught you.'

'No, you can't,' says Dark Star. 'My name is Hassan. Your daughter is very safe with me.'

'Is she?' He looks at me, questioning me also. 'Louise?'

'I'm fine, Dad,' I tell him. 'I am very safe. What can happen to me here?'

Coral whispers again. Then she speaks.

'There's been a shooting in Munich,' she says. 'There's been a bomb in Bologna. Where is Bologna?'

'In Italy,' Dad says. 'A long way from here, Coral.'

'Ah. The world seems to be in a state of collapse.'

'Does it?' I say.

'Yes. Don't you think the news is awful?'

'I don't listen to it.'

'There is so much death and destruction.'

'I think there has been always death and destruction,' says Dark Star. 'Civilisation is always about to fall. So there has been a shooting and a bomb. But how many car crashes have there been today? How many people have been killed by cancer? And why do we talk only about the bad things?'

'That's right,' says Dad. 'The news is skewed. It doesn't tell us how many babies have been born today.' He puts his arm around the woman's waist. 'It doesn't tell us how many women and men have fallen in love today.'

'But there are bad guys,' the woman says. 'So many of them who want to harm us.'

'Terrorists,' says Dark Star. 'Suicide bombers. Maniacs with guns and knives. Is that what you mean?'

'Yes,' says the woman. 'There was a stabbing in London just as I arrived.'

'Do you think I am one of those people? Because of Syria and my skin. That I was in

London with my knife? That I am a terrorist come to Lindisfarne with dreams of slaughter?'

She gazes at him.

'Of course she doesn't think that,' says Dad. 'Do you, Coral?'

She shakes her head.

'No,' she says. 'I don't think that.'

But her gaze rests on Dark Star, and I see that she could quite easily think that.

Then she says no again, smiles sweetly at me, and they turn away and walk hand-in-hand through the air and light.

'Is true, of course.' he says. 'The world is dangerous, has always been and always will be dangerous. How can it be otherwise when there are human beings in it?'

'Hassan?' I say.

'Yes. Hassan.'

'And where is your father, Hassan?'

'Ah. Where is he? Let us walk through the shadows and the light.'

He puts his rucksack on his back.

'Let us walk,' he says, 'through the living and the dead.'

*

My phone buzzes. I take it out. Becca.

It is pouring here. Trust the Lakes. And the tent is useless. And we are hungbliddyover (again). Xx

I laugh.

'My friends,' I say to Hassan.

I text back.

Poor souls. Good weather here. Come here and we'll have some fun. Xx

What about your dad? xx

He's in bliddy love. Xx

?? xx

!! xx

'They miss you?' says Hassan.

'We miss each other.'

Becca: *No, we'll stay. Have hitched up with some German lasses and some very bonny Swedish lads.*

Xx The world's yer oyster, lass. xx

Our oyster. YOLO. xx

*

His feet are so silent as we walk, as if there is no weight to him. I start to tell him about the civilisation that existed here, the art that was created here. I tell him that it is a place of pilgrimage.

'I know that, Louise. I too am on pilgrimage.'

'You?'

'My father told me stories when I was a boy about an island far off in the north, a place of icy water and cold blue sky and fish that leap and flowers that bloom behind walls in a garden and of cold bright air and of ground that is cool and gentle against the feet.'

'He knew Lindisfarne?'

'Yes.'

'He came here?'

'He came in 2003, when I was a boy, before Syria became a place of destruction, bombs and death.'

We walk on, past the calm garden, past the castle bulked high against the southern sky.

'And it was he,' says Hassan, 'who told me

about boats turned upside down and made into houses.'

'I saw you go to them, as if you knew them. It was like you'd been looking for them.'

'They were something I had always known. I used to dream of them, of sailing in one upside down across the stars.'

'That's what I did! That's what I do!'

'Yes. I saw your drawing on the wall. You did it when you were a little girl, I think.'

He quickens his step. We walk further, beyond the castle and the garden, into the wilder parts of the place I thought I knew so well.

And I want to take his hand, to enter this strange new place along with him.

A black jet streaks low over Longstone Lighthouse. We hear its distant subdued roar.

'Such noises are heard each day over Syria,' says Hassan. 'They are accompanied by the noises of bombs falling, of sirens, of people screaming.'

I don't know what to say.

'It must be terrible,' I mutter blandly.

'My father was a librarian,' he says.

'You said he was a tent-maker.'

'No. His father was, and his father before that, and his brother. The tent-making made the family rich. My father went to university in Damascus and he became a librarian. He cared for ancient manuscripts.'

'He must have been a clever man.'

Bland again, stupid again.

'Yes. Of course. And he wanted to see the great manuscripts of the world. So he travelled to your country to see the great Lindisfarne Gospels in London. He saw how beautiful they are. He saw how wonderful it was that such pages were saved from the destroyers. He said that civilisation is carried in the pages of such books.'

'And he came here?'

'Yes, to the place where such a masterpiece was made.'

The skylarks continue to sing. In the water there are seals, their heads bobbing above the water. Beyond the seals, the sea and the coastline stretch southward. The great castle of Bamburgh towers on its rock above its beach. Beyond that, sea and sky merge with each other. Beyond that, Newcastle, London, Milan, Syria, the world, the universe. We come to the place where I saw the deer. He pauses in his walking as he tells his father's tale.

'He came to Lindisfarne only for one day. It was a day of brilliant sunshine and soft breezes. I was his little boy in Syria, six years old. I remember that I missed him so. "Where is Daddy?" I asked my mother every morning, every night. "He is in the far-off north," she told me. "Will he not be very cold there?" I would ask, and she would smile. "No," she told me. "In those places they wear hats and coats and they carry umbrellas because of the rain." So I had a picture of my father on a cold rock beneath an umbrella with the rain pouring down on him. But the day that he came here, he told me, was very beautiful and very sunlit – a day just like today, in fact. He told me that he came on a bus, that he waited for the shining water to fall before he could be driven across. He told me also of many other places, much more grand – the towers and cathedrals and cities of Europe. My father told me of these wonders, and of the whole world, but he said that this place, the most northern of the places he came to, was the most peaceful of all. And he sent me postcards from everywhere so that I could see his words were true.'

'And you still have the postcards?'

'Yes. They bear his writing, and they are safe, and are with my mother. And he took photographs as he travelled.'

'You have those, too?'

'Yes. Of course. They are very precious, Louise. We brought them from Syria. We saved them from the bombs, as we saved the postcards.'

There are howls that I know must be the bare-chested boys somewhere in the north of the island. And another gentler howling that might be the sound of singing seals. We walk on and come to the dunes, to the beach, the pale sand, the dark wet rocks, the gently turning sea.

Smoke is rising from among the dunes at the far end of the beach.

We sit in a soft fold of the dunes and look out together across the great sea. Other islands, the Farnes, stretch towards the horizon. I feel my mother's shade close by and I am pleased by that. Hassan is very quiet now and I know that he needs to be silent. I take out my notebook and begin to write, word by word, step by step, a record of our walk. I draw the castle, the garden, the seals, the skylarks. I take a breath and begin to draw Hassan himself, his profile against the sea and sky. I write his name: DARK STAR. HASSAN. I draw the dark star at the centre of his chest. I draw the dark ashen star that is high on my chest.

'I feel him here,' says Hassan at last. 'He is in the air and light as well as in my memory.'

'That's good,' I whisper.

'I feel my mother, too. She calls out for me. She tells me that I have reached Lindisfarne and now it is time for me to go back to her.'

He looks at the pages I am creating.

He turns his face from me and towards the blue sky. 'I will return soon,' he says, as if his mother is able to hear him.

Then he talks again.

'My father had only a few hours here, between the falling and the rising of the tide. Perhaps it was like life itself – a few moments of great beauty and grace before we must depart. And from that time the thing he remembered most of all was an upturned boat with a little girl outside it.'

'A little girl?'

'Yes. A little girl with her mother and her father. She was dressed in red and white. The door to the boat was wide open. There was fish cooking on a fire.'

I hold my breath. I cannot speak.

'My father was a shy man,' Hassan continues. 'He told me that he wished he had spoken to the people outside the upturned boat that day. But all he did was to pass by slowly, to glimpse the shade inside the boat, to catch the scent of the fish cooking, to hear the father's laughter, to hear the singing of the mother, and to see the girl dancing. He said it was a glimpse of what could be heaven, Louise, here on this little earth.'

'So he saw me? He saw all of us?'

'Yes. And I did, too.'

Hassan opens his rucksack and reaches inside.

'My father paused, Louise. He had his camera with him. He raised it and he said he saw that these people wouldn't mind. And he took this photograph.'

And he takes it from an envelope, the photograph of me as a little girl, me with my family as we were before, outside the shed made from an upturned boat on Lindisfarne. There we are, the three of us together. I'm dancing. Mum is clapping as I dance. Dad has turned his smiling face to look at the photographer. And I hold it in my hands and I hear my mother's singing and the laughter of my father and the skipping of my feet upon the grass and sand, and I can't speak as

I stare and stare through all the years between.

*

Perhaps I gaze at it for a minute, perhaps for an hour. I can't be certain. Hassan sits silent and still beside me until he tells me:

'It is for you,' he says.

'But it's yours.'

'It is a copy. Just as my father made copies of the ancient manuscripts he cared for in Syria. It is a way of protecting them, of making sure that at least the memory of them cannot be destroyed.'

'What happened to your father, Hassan?'

'Death happened,' he says.

'Oh, Hassan.'

'We were fleeing Palmyra two years ago, we were fleeing war, we were fleeing bullets and bombs and stupid destruction. We were heading for the sea. My father said that across the sea in Europe we would be safe and free. But Death is hungry and Destruction is determined and it does not like its intended victims to get away. A man blew himself to bits by a roadside as we

96

passed by. And he blew some of us to bits along with him.'

'Oh, Hassan.'

'I saw my father's legs in the roadway. I saw his head in a ditch.'

'Oh, Hassan.'

'That is what Destruction is. It wants to tear us from each other. It wants to tear apart the body. It wants for nothing to be safely held together, nothing to be safe.'

'Oh, Hassan.'

I put my arm across his shoulder. He leans his head on me.

'I feel him here, in this place,' he says. 'I feel the man who took the photograph, who saw you as a little girl. I feel him breathing this air, hearing these birds, wandering by this beach, knowing heaven, knowing peace. That's why I came here to Lindisfarne, to feel him in the place he said was the most peaceful in the world, to look upon the same things he looked upon.'

And there's a scream that crashes us out of

our memories and dreams. It comes from in the dunes, from where the smoke is rising, further along the beach. It's an inhuman scream of loss and terror. We gather our things, stand up and hurry towards it. I'm scared and tentative. Hassan is all alert. We walk up into the high dunes, and our feet slip and slither on the soft sand. We tug on the tough marram grass and we haul ourselves onward, upward. Skylarks dash from cover and rush singing into the sky. The screaming gets weaker, turns into a squeak, a gasp, then just nothing. We head towards the silence. Then there's someone weeping. A boy's high voice yelling, 'You shouldn't have done it! You shouldn't have done it!' And then we come to the edge of a deep depression in the dunes. Down there on the soft sand are the three bare-chested boys. A fire is burning. There is a deer in the sand, a young one, a child. Anderson is leaning over it, hacking at it with his knife, yanking at it with his hand, he's trying to saw off its head.

One of the boys sees us. The look he gives is

filled with horror, fear, deep humiliation. He is shuddering violently. His eyes appeal to us to come, to rescue him, to change what has been done.

Then Anderson sees us. He sneers and snarls.

'Just in time for dinner!' he says. 'Venison stew, anybody?'

He stabs and hacks and carves.

Hassan slides down towards him on the sand.

The two friends back away, cowering. Both of them are weeping.

'We telt him no,' says one of them.

'We telt him stop,' says the other.

'It wasn't us,' they say together.

'Wimps,' says Anderson. 'How do you expect to get some meat if you're not prepared to kill?'

There's blood all over his hands and arms, smeared on his chest, spattered on his face.

'Stop it,' says Hassan.

'Too late to stop now.' Anderson lifts the deer's half-severed head and lets it fall. 'See? Very dead. Very very dead.'

He continues to hack and stab.

'Stop it,' says Hassan again.

Anderson swipes his bloody hand across his face.

'And what's it got to do with you?'

Hassan steps around the fire.

Anderson raises the knife and watches him come.

'You're a monster!' I yell.

He laughs.

'That's great, coming from a savage's girlfriend.'

He stands, turns from the deer, points the knife at Hassan.

'What are you?' he snarls. 'Savage. Wild man, refubliddygee. Get back home to where you come from. Coming here to chop our heads off and stab us and shoot us and blow us all to bliddy bits.'

'I am a human being, like you,' says Hassan. 'I am a creature like this deer. I am a thing of earth just like this sand. Put the knife down.'

Anderson sneers.

'A creature like this deer. A thing of earth just like this sand.'

He waves the knife before him.

The air shudders as an unseen jet screeches low above the sea.

He beckons Hassan towards him.

'Howay, then, creature like this deer. Come and see what you can do.'

Hassan doesn't move.

I slide down the slope of sand.

I crouch by the dead animal. I put my hand flat against its body. I feel the smooth hair, the flesh and bone beneath. It's still warm. Just a few minutes into death. Its dead eye is open, and it reflects the bright sky. Poor tender lost thing. Is anything left of your spirit, of your soul? Yesterday I saw your body arching as you leapt between the earth and sky. Does your spirit still leap? Do you still step through the places where my mother steps? Do you now walk with the dead among the living?

I run my palm across its still and tender body.

I tell Anderson to put the knife away.

He laughs and then he's at me. I realise that I have put the notebook and photograph down on to the sand. He takes them, lifts them.

'What's this?' he hisses. 'What bliddy crap is this?'

I lurch towards him. Hassan steps forward. But Anderson holds the book and photograph above the fire, daring us to come closer.

'Don't,' I tell him.

'Give them back,' says Hassan.

'Are they so precious?' asks Anderson.

'You wouldn't understand them,' I tell him.

'What are they? Love letters? Tender tales of sweetness and joy?'

He flicks through the pages. He stares at the photograph.

He holds them above the flames.

'They're civilisation,' I say.

'Civilisation!' he mocks. 'Messy pages and a stupid photograph?'

'Yes. A person who could do that to a deer wouldn't understand.'

'Ah, poor me. I'm just so thick. So thick, maybe I should just let your civilisation go up in flames.'

'You can burn it,' I tell him. 'But you can't destroy it. I'll write it and draw it all again.'

I shift towards him.

'I'll write it better,' I say. 'That's what civilisation is. It keeps on being recreated. Monsters like you can't hold it back.'

'Then let the monster make it burn.'

He drops them. I dive towards them but already they're burning, smoking, smouldering. I pluck them out, drop them on the sand, blow on them, pat them with my fingers, put out the flames. There's blood on them, soot on them.

Now Hassan is with Anderson, struggling for the knife. It's easy for Hassan to gain the upper hand. He's agile, quick and strong, and Anderson just seems a brute.

And Anderson is down in the sand and Hassan

is kneeling over him and he has the knife held high. And suddenly Anderson is terrified by what seems about to come.

'I am Hassan,' says Hassan. 'I am from Syria. I am from where civilisation has been destroyed. I have seen what war is. I saw my father's legs in a roadway and his head in a ditch. I have seen babies drowned. I have been brutalised, Anderson. I have been terrorised. I have seen much worse than this dead deer. Does that worry you?'

Anderson gasps and squirms.

'You should be worried,' says Hassan. 'I have seen worse monsters than you, Anderson. I have seen what nobody should see. I have felt what nobody should feel. I know what nobody should know. What would it be to me to see this knife in your throat? Nothing. What would it be for me to see you as dead as this deer? Nothing. What would it be to me to see you lying dead among the jetsam on the beach?'

Anderson gurgles, whimpers.

'Nothing,' says Hassan. 'It would be nothing.

It is how all things end – lives, civilisations, planets. What would it be to the universe if I plunged this knife into your throat, if I turned this stupid boy, this stupid Anderson to nothing? Nothing, Anderson. Nothing at all. So maybe it is what I should do.'

Hassan holds the knife against Anderson's throat.

He leans down close to Anderson's eyes, to his ears, to his brutalised mind.

And Anderson gurgles and gasps and weeps and begs for mercy.

'This is what civilisation is,' says Hassan. 'It is the power to take photographs and to write words. It is the power to love the beauty of the world and to love all living things. It is the power to move at liberty through the world. It is also the power to take life.'

He presses the knife to Anderson's skin.

'No!' I gasp. 'No, Hassan!'

He ignores me. He concentrates his gaze, his words, his breath, on Anderson.

'And it is the power not to kill,' he says. 'It is the power to let you go. Shall I let you go?'

'Yes,' gasps Anderson. 'Yes. Please let me go!'

'No,' says Hassan. 'Don't beg. Don't plead. Go away from the island. Don't return until you've changed. Will you do that?'

'Yes.'

And Hassan stands back, and Anderson squirms away across the sand, disappears into the dunes.

The objects of civilisation in my hands are cooling. I scrape away the charred edges. I wipe away the ash. They are damaged, mutilated, but they're saved.

The boys left behind are small, timid, young.

'What are your names?' says Hassan.

'Michael.'

'Chris.'

Chris is sobbing.

'What will you do now?' asks Hassan.

'Go home,' says Michael.

'Yes,' says Hassan. 'You must go home. You

must know how lucky you are to go home. You must be kind. You must not do harm to the world. You must not make war. Do you understand?'

'Yes,' they whisper.

Do they? Who knows? Hassan leans down and presses the knife blade hard against a stone until it breaks.

'Do you understand?' he says again.

'Yes.'

Michael puts his arm around his friend. He guides him away. We lose sight of them in the dunes.

We throw sand on to the fire to put it out.

Tears are falling from my eyes.

'Sometimes I despair,' I tell Hassan.

'No,' he answers. 'Don't despair. Despair is what the barbarians want. Never give it to them.'

Then he lifts the deer and rests it across his shoulders. Its legs hang down across his chest. Its lovely head rests against his throat. Blood trickles from it on to him.

*

We head back to the beach. I find that Hassan is holding my hand in his. I continue crying. We step out from the dunes. Then I see them, through my tears, out beyond the breaking waves, out where the endless sea is calm.

The whales, a family of them, rising and falling in the icy sea.

We stand watching, in excitement. A family hurries on to the beach, a father, a mother, a young child. They see the deer on Hassan's shoulders but now isn't the time to talk about that.

'We saw them when we were by the castle!' says the mother.

'I saw them,' says the girl.

'We thought it was impossible,' says the father. 'We thought it must be seals or seaweed or just the waves.'

'But it was whales!' says the girl. 'Whales! Whales! Whales!'

'Whales!' says Hassan.

We all watch together as the whales show themselves to us, as if in celebration of great freedom, great joy, great celebration of this world, its great beauty and of all of its inhabitants.

We see their great bodies rising from the waves and diving down again. Rising and falling from the water to the air and back again. And then they disappear, lost in the endless sea.

We all sigh and smile and know that we have been privileged.

Then the little girl turns to us.

'I said they were whales,' she says. 'Didn't I, Mummy? Didn't I, Dad?'

She gazes at Hassan.

'What is that?'

'A deer. It is dead. It was killed by a boy who did not understand what he was doing.'

She reaches up and tenderly touches it.

'Poor deer,' she says. 'It's very beautiful.'

'Yes,' says Hassan.

'Where are you from?' she asks.

'I am from Syria. My name is Hassan.'

'My name is Emily. Is it nice there?'

'It is very beautiful. It was and it will be.'

'Is it as beautiful as here?'

'Yes, it is. But you must go there one day and see it for yourself.'

'I will,' says the girl. 'And I will remember meeting you.'

'Good,' says Hassan. 'That is good, Emily. You will take Lindisfarne and the deer and the whales with you.'

And he crouches down and lifts some sand and holds it in his hands and manipulates it and then opens his hands again and there is a tiny golden metal bird there with its wings outstretched.

'This is for you, Emily,' he says.

He holds it out towards her and she takes it in her small young hands.

'It's warm,' she says.

'Ah yes, because it has just this minute been created.'

She laughs. She says that she will keep it for ever.

'That's good,' says Hassan. 'I will always think of you, caring for this lovely bird.'

And then her mother asks if she can photograph us all. So we stand together, Hassan, the deer, me, the father, and Emily with the magic bird held high in her hands. And the photograph is created, the four of us with the castle and the sea behind and the endless sky above, the photograph that will be seen all through the years as Emily grows into a woman, the photograph that will help this moment and this day live for ever more.

And we say our farewells and we move again, away from the silent beach, past the castle and the garden, away from the wilder places, back towards the harbour and the upturned boats.

*

There are people who stare and groan in disgust and mutter as we walk back past the garden and the castle towards the harbour. Outside the upturned boatshed, Hassan lifts the deer from his shoulders and rests it on the sandy turf.

One of the lobster fishermen comes to us and stands there and looks.

I tell him what happened and who did this thing.

He tells us that the police have been called, that they'll be here from Berwick in the morning when the tide is down.

He says he has seen the bare-chested boys. They are bad news, he says. I say they didn't understand what they were doing.

'I wonder whether the other deer will realise,' he muses. 'What do you think?' he asks us.

'Yes,' I say. 'I think the deer will know in some way that one of them is missing. Maybe they'll feel the young one still walking by their side.'

He nods his head in agreement, and then he leaves.

I write the story of the deer and the whales. I draw the boys by the fire with the dead creature. I draw Emily and the whales.

'I will send you another copy of the photograph,' says Hassan, 'once I am back in Milan with my mother.'

'Thank you.'

'Maybe you will come to see us there, Louise.'

I think of the travelling I will do with Becca and Gem.

'Yes,' I tell him. 'We'll keep in touch. I'll travel to Milan.'

I look out across the sea towards the horizon. I look into my world of possibilities.

I draw myself and my friends with rucksacks on our backs and smiles of excitement on our faces.

And Dad comes, with his woman. We tell them, too, about the deer and the boys.

'I wondered,' he says. 'We saw Anderson. He was on the causeway, running as the tide came in. Stupid fool. I yelled at him to come back but he took no notice. Just went on running, then wading. As if he could beat the sea. He'll be OK. He got as far as the refuge hut. We saw him climbing the steps up to it.' He laughs. 'Maybe there he'll see the stupidity of what's been done.'

Dad and his woman sit together on the sandy turf, close to the deer. They hold hands. I open my notebook and take out the charred and damaged photograph. I brush away more crumbs of ash. Each of us – Dad, Mum, me – is still decipherable despite the scars.

'Look at this,' I say to Dad. 'Look what Hassan brought us.'

He takes it. He looks into the mystery of it.

'But how?' he whispers.

Hassan smiles and tells the tale.

'Do you remember it happening?' I ask.

Dad's eyes glaze over. He closes them. He searches his mind, his past. It was a fleeting thing, a mundane thing.

He catches his breath.

'Oh my goodness, I do,' he murmurs. Tears show in his eyes as he opens them again and gazes at Hassan, at me. 'It was unusual. A man, a Middle Eastern man, alone on Lindisfarne with a camera. He took the picture quickly, as if we might not approve, or …'

'He was a shy man,' says Hassan.

'Ah, of course. Your mum wanted to call him back, Louise, to ask him to take another, one in which we looked into the camera for him. I remember what she said: he took it because we look so happy. What did he do next? I can't recall. Wandered on, as tourists do.'

He looks at the photograph again.

'Because we were so happy,' he repeats. 'And your father now, Hassan?'

'He was killed in Syria, as we escaped.'

And Hassan repeats the short tale.

*

We all sit there as the sun continues to fall. I feel strangely at peace, there on the island outside the shed with these people and the deer. The skylarks are singing, the gulls calling, the sea turning. I sense Mum watching us from the spaces between the boatsheds.

I even look fondly at Dad's woman, at Coral.

They must sense that, because soon she gives us the outline of a tale of her own. A tale of Vietnam.

'I'm going there to search for my mother,' she says. 'My father was a soldier in the war. I never knew him. I don't know Vietnam. I was brought to the States when I was two. My mother gave me to some nuns and begged them to find me a better life. I'm so scared about getting there at last. Maybe there'll be no one. Maybe there will be.'

I ask some questions and I hear her stories: a baby left on the steps of a convent in war-ravaged Saigon, with a note pinned to her chest asking that she be given a better life. I hear about an orphanage in Missouri. I begin to see her, to know her. She's no longer just the woman with the slender legs and the low-cut top, seducer of my father.

'I'm so glad I found myself here,' she says. 'I'm so happy to have met you all on Lindisfarne.'

Lindisfarne. It's weird that war and peace, life

and death, the disappearance and discovery of parents from all around the world, bitter loss and new-found love are focused here in this little group of people in this little place.

But that'd be the same everywhere, wouldn't it?

That'd be the same in any group of people gathered in any place at all.

I laugh inside. Maybe Dad and Coral really are falling in love. I smile at him. I shrug.

Soon they rise together from the sandy turf. They walk away with hands joined, like teenagers. I catch a glimpse of Mum. I roll my eyes, I laugh, I sigh, I shake my head, I shrug, like I'm the parent watching the young one leave.

I ask Hassan if he'd like to sleep in the cottage tonight. He says no. The upturned boat is what he has been searching for. He'll sleep in there again. I bring a bowl of water from the cottage so that he can wash the blood from himself. We eat fish and bread again. We drink red wine and water as the sun falls and the moon rises over the sea. After a time, we move closer and we kiss.

When we go into the upturned boat together we take the deer in with us. Don't want it to be left outside to feed rats and owls. I see Mum silhouetted against the moon, standing in the shallows, as she watches me shut the door.

I hear her gentle whisper on the gentle breeze.

'Good night, my darling girl.'

I am happy. I am a baby, a toddler, a girl, a woman. I am Island. I am Lindisfarne. Everything comes together inside me. I know that I will go to Palmyra one day when peace has come, just as people come to Lindisfarne, just as Coral will go to Vietnam. War is not for ever. Peace will come. Civilisation will endure. The destroyers will be overcome. The human heart will love and thrive.

We lie on the sand in the upturned boat together, Hassan and I.

We kiss and smile.

Soon the boat rises. It carries us from the island into the night sky. It carries us up beyond the turning lighthouse and the gleaming moon.

And all of us are in it, all the living and the dead, all carried upside down through the astounding stars.

Read on for an exclusive extract from **Orangeboy**,
the brilliant debut novel from Patrice Lawrence.

I pulled myself on to the bench and slumped down, clinging to the plastic. Adrenaline and cortisol had kicked at my brain and run away again. I had nothing left to help me move.

The bus doors puffed open. 'Marlon?' Wheels and feet. 'Marlon!'

I frowned, trying to open my good eye wide.

'Tish …'

'Jesus, Marlon! What happened?'

I tried to speak; my throat still wouldn't work. I managed to stand up, one hand on Tish's shoulder and the other one on the side of the bus shelter. That dark splodge on the ground, was that my blood? I touched my face. The cut felt split open.

Tish said, 'Can you walk?'

No! Can't you feel me shaking?

'Come on, Marlon! Just a few steps, right?'

One foot after the other, each step a jab in my gut. We crossed the road, me leaning heavily against Tish's shoulders.

'Where are your keys?' she said.

'Pocket.'

She fished inside my jacket, pulled them out and opened the door.

'Oh Jesus,' she said. 'Oh God.'

Somewhere in the back of my throat words started, but stayed stuck there. Cane Row must have had a plan – mash it up and mash it hard. They'd charged through the house like a damn army, kicking around our shoes, pulling down our coats, throwing all our pictures on the floor. I looked at myself, Year Nine, with my face stamped in. And my grandma, a year before she died, glass cracks cutting through her cheek.

I had to hold the wall to help me into the sitting room. They must have known this place was special, because they'd put in the work. They'd found my old kids' encyclopaedias, Dad's atlases, the posh Dickens collection Mum bought herself last Christmas. They'd bounced them like tennis balls and then just ripped the pages out. I picked up *Oliver Twist*. Its spine was all floppy and bent.

Tish was shaking her head, looking ready to cry.

I said, 'I'll get them.'

Tish looked at me. 'We need to call the police, Marlon.'

'No.'

'Yes, Marlon. You're not Andre. You're not a gangsta, remember?'

Yeah, I remembered. Because if I was, I wouldn't be standing here now. I'd be on the phone, gathering my own army, priming my weapons. This was beef, proper beef. When it happened, your mates came with you to sort it out.

Tish picked up an armful of our crushed books. 'This must be them, Marlon. Just give them the phone, all right?'

'No.'

'Things are getting too hot.'

'I haven't got it any more.'

'What?'

'I'm going to check upstairs.'

I pulled myself up along the banister. A mob of mini-men were setting off bangers in my head, one step, one explosion. All the upstairs doors were flung open. I could see into Mum's room; nothing looked disturbed. But my room …

The duvet and sheet were pulled off my bed and they'd emptied out the drawers into a mountain of pillows and covers. All my books, music, school stuff, everything, was piled up on top like the start of a bloody great bonfire. The vinyl, Lonnie Liston Smith, George Benson, The Jones Girls, flung across the room. Brothers Johnson, smashed.

'Look what that girl dropped you in!' Tish's eyes were wide and furious.

Read on to find out what happens next.
Orangeboy is out now in paperback and ebook.

BOOK IN FOR YOUR NEW ADVENTURE TODAY

CELEBRATING WORLD BOOK DAY 20 2 MARCH 2017

---

3 brilliant ways to continue YOUR reading adventure

1 VISIT YOUR LOCAL BOOKSHOP

Your go-to destination for awesome reading recommendations and events with your favourite authors and illustrators.

 Booksellers.org.uk/ bookshopsearch

2 JOIN YOUR LOCAL LIBRARY

Browse and borrow from a huge selection of books, get expert ideas of what to read next, and take part in wonderful family reading activities – all for FREE!

FIND YOUR LOCAL LIBRARY **Findalibrary.co.uk**

3 DISCOVER A WORLD OF STORIES ONLINE

 32 podcasts to try

Stuck for ideas of what to read next? Plug yourself in to our brilliant new podcast library! Sample a world of amazing books, brought to life by amazing storytellers. **worldbookday.com**

HAPPY BIRTHDAY WORLD BOOK DAY!

Let's celebrate . . .

Can you believe this year is our **20th birthday** – and thanks to you, as well as our amazing authors, illustrators, booksellers, librarians and teachers, there's SO much to celebrate!

Did you know that since WORLD BOOK DAY began in 1997, we've given away over **275 million book tokens**? WOW! We're delighted to have brought so many books directly into the hands of millions of children and young people just like you, with a gigantic assortment of fun activities and events and resources and quizzes and dressing-up and games too – we've even broken a **Guinness World Record**!

Whether you love discovering books that make you **laugh**, CRY, *hide under the covers* or **drive your imagination wild**, with WORLD BOOK DAY, there's always something for everyone to choose–as well as ideas for exciting new books to try at bookshops, libraries and schools everywhere.

And as a small charity, we couldn't do it without a lot of help from our friends in the publishing industry and our brilliant sponsor, NATIONAL BOOK TOKENS. Hip-hip hooray to them and three cheers to you, our readers and everyone else who has joined us over the last 20 years to make WORLD BOOK DAY happen.

Happy Birthday to us – and happy reading to you!

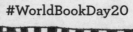

#WorldBookDay20